MW01386182

Mechanic's Wife

Author

MARION MUTALA

Silver Medal Award Winner

2016 Destiny Whispers Extraordinary Moment Creative Writing Contest

The Mechanic's Wife
Text © Marion Mutala, 2020
Illustrations © Olha Tkachenko,2020

FIRST EDITION / Award Winning Destiny Whispers Publisher, LLC
ISBN-13: 978-1-943504-27-5 (softcover)
AMAZON EDITION EBOOK ISBN-10 :1-943504-27-X
December 28,2016
SECOND EDITION/December/2020
ISBN: 978-1-7773713-0-2
Library and Archives Canada Cataloguing in Publication

Author Photo © Bruce Blom
Border Design ©Kara Obrigewitsch
Creative Consultant: Martin Hryniuk
Edited by Angie Wollbaum, Ed Anderson
Layout & Design: Olha Tkachenko
Printed in Canada

Millennium Marketing
Saskatoon, SK.
www.babasbabushka.ca

Other books by Marion Mutala
Children's Books
Baba's Babushka: A Magical Ukrainian Christmas

Baba's Babushka: A Magical Ukrainian Easter

Baba's Babushka: A Magical Ukrainian Wedding

Kohkum's Babushka: A Magical Metis/ Ukrainian Tale

Baba's Babushka: A Magical Ukrainian Journey

Grateful

More Baba's, Please!

My Buddy, Dido!

Young Adult
My Dearest Dido-The Holodomor Story

Poetry
Ukrainian Daughter's Dance

Fiction
The Time for Peace is Now

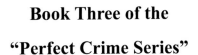
Book Three of the

"Perfect Crime Series"

Books one and two are still

under investigation

Dedication

The year 2020 sounded so exciting. Then the COVID crisis hit. Let us remember and thank all the frontline workers in all professions that are taking care and helping provide for us during this difficult time. Prayers go out to those families that have lost loved ones due to COVID 19.

Let us also remember the refugees in the world, especially women and children, struggling to find a home and receive the necessary basic human rights of safety, security and freedom and the opportunity to receive food, clothing, shelter, healthcare, and education.

From the Author

This novel is entirely a work of fiction. The names and characters portrayed are completely imaginative. Any resemblance to actual persons, events, and places are purely coincidentally. However, some places in Saskatchewan do exist like: Hafford, Saskatchewan, Crooked Trees or Crooked Bush, (near Alticane, Saskatchewan) Redberry Lake, Saskatchewan, Kenaston, Saskatchewan, Saskatoon, Saskatchewan, and the Ukrainian Gala with performers in Regina, Saskatchewan.

Former Premier Brad Wall declared 2016 the year to recognize and honour "Ukrainians in Saskatchewan" for their dedicated work, great service, and contributions to the province.

My late mother, Sophie Mutala (Dubyk) grew up near Hafford and my late grandparents; Tessie Woznakowski and Stefan Dubyk emigrated from Ukraine in 1912 and 1911 during the first wave of Ukrainian immigration to Canada. They farmed in the Hafford area and are buried at Hafford. When my mother, married my father, August Mutala, she moved to a farm in the Hanley/Kenaston area. I grew up in that area with my nine siblings and now live in Saskatoon. I picked these places for my story as they are near and dear to my heart.

Chapter 1

SLEEPLESS

2:13 a.m.

"Aaauurrgghh." Frustration, bordering anger was the feeling DD had as she clenched her right fist and lightly hit the bedpost beside her. Wiggling her torso, lifting her left leg to roll over, now laying on her right side, DD could not sleep.

What was it about solving this case? Her mind kept going over the facts. The man, the woman, the perfect crime. Rolling about as she thought, writhing around on the queen-size bed, something bothered her about this evidence. The photographs taken in the garage, the floor, the ramps, the leg cast, her keen sense, and Ukrainian nose indicated something was wrong. What? What was it?

"*Bozhe*, my God," when frustrated she returned to her mother's Ukrainian language as certain phrases remained from her childhood. Tossing and turning, someone should write a song about that. Mind over matter.

"Sleep, come to me gracious, lady."

Flipping onto her back, she placed her right hand on her flat, toned, and tanned stomach, while rubbing her left hand across her ribcage. She wriggled her head to the left and pushed down on the pillow to create a comfortable nest on her bed. Sleep evaded her, something common when working on a tough case. Lying there, eyes wide open; mind wandering, she again visualized the crime scene. DD knew she needed to find the missing piece of this puzzle to complete the entire picture.

Where was the key to unlock this door?

What was she overlooking?

Yoi, it was driving her crazy!

5:17 am

Her nightgown now removed, lay in a heap beside the bed. The covers tangled inside her long legs as the soft light of day illuminated the room. Still unable to doze, DD's mind kept churning. There was something bothering her about his body. The way he was positioned on the floor, that was very odd indeed.

Why was his hand in his pocket? He should have been reaching out or protecting himself. His hand: that was it. It had to be. His hand was in his pocket the whole time. Why would he have his hand in his pocket while he was lying on the floor? That just didn't make any sense.

Again, she pondered.

"Unless, —AHA."

DD smiled, stretched like a feline, sighed an audible moan, hummed a *kolomiyka* Ukrainian dance tune, and kicked the covers to the floor. The puzzle was finally put together. Finding the lost piece, she could rest at last.

"*Chiki, chiki,* just you wait and see. Wow, I know exactly how it happened," she murmured sleepily.

Sleep, precious sleep came at last.

It should have been "the perfect crime." He just about got away with it, almost—except for DD, detective extraordinaire. Another case solved. What a super sleuth! *Duzhe dobre*, very good. Girl power!

Canada's famous female Ukrainian detective is no longer just a private eye. Today, she is well known in the public eye as a star pupil and renowned private investigator. Perhaps, it is because she rarely sleeps until the felon is apprehended.

Ah, but that's another chapter.

Chapter 2

DD

DD's younger years were blah. Known as Deirdre, she was a thin underdeveloped, disproportional, gaunt, beanpole with knobby knees. She was often picked on, pointed at, or ridiculed openly in school. Standing 177.5 centimeters she was not DD then, but only plain Deirdre. Gaudy, frumpy, Deirdre. With mousey blonde, straight, stringy hair, hazel-blue eyes, thin lips, and high cheekbones, attractive was not a word describing Deirdre's appearance.

Lacking self-esteem like many teenagers, she generally dressed according to her feelings. Wearing a second hand, dark green pullover sweater that fit a couple sizes too large was common. With fuzzy wool balls clinging, her printed cotton dress hung almost to her ankles. Preferring longer clothes, her old, dirty, greying, white socks would not be noticed bunched above her outdated Converse grass stained running shoes.

Dowdy was the best way to describe Deirdre then. Some of the school's jocks demeaningly referred to her as DD. As she was soon forgotten, the term did not catch on. Ironically, she liked the name DD and wanted the tag to stay as she felt it fit her imaginary personality.

Life was not easy, having experienced many misfortunes. The teasing and bullying at school were harsh due to Deirdre's geeky bookworm portrayal. The lack of friendship or opportunities to showcase her superior intelligence other than through schoolwork was noticeable in the small village of Hafford, Saskatchewan, a Ukrainian village, located about a one-hour drive from Saskatoon, Saskatchewan.

Hafford, 96 kilometers away from Saskatoon was often referred to as the Ukrainian capital of Saskatchewan, as even its *Cyrillic* street signs were written in Ukrainian.

It seemed wherever DD went somebody knew or had a Ukrainian connection to the place; a village of about 400 people. Hafford was close to the "Crooked Trees" or "Crooked Bush" as some people call it, near Alticane, Saskatchewan. It was a strange phenomenon, a group of trees on a farmer's field that grew in all directions and look like hearts and all kinds of interesting images. Even the University of Saskatchewan scientists cannot explain why the trees grow that way. Maybe aliens, it has been suggested.

"Sure aliens, right, *dummkopfs*, dummies!" DD always said.

Hafford, was one of the earliest and largest Ukrainian settlements in Saskatchewan. Years ago, in 1891, Ukrainians first started emigrating from now Ukraine to Canada and many settled in this area. Many tourists loved to visit this beautiful place, near Redberry Lake, Saskatchewan, about 13 kilometers near Hafford as it has been declared a UNESCO Biosphere Reserve.

The village also has an annual, "Summer Sizzle" a Ukrainian festival of fun, singing and Ukrainian dancing. Many people love to come experience or share in Ukrainian traditional culture of eating *pyrohy*, dumplings filled with potatoes, cottage cheese, or *holubtsi*, cabbage rolls, soured cabbage leaves filled with rice, and *kovbasa* or Ukrainian garlic sausage, some of DD's favorite food. A recent survey in western Canada deemed *varenyky* or *perogies* the number one favorite food in Canada. DD's mouth just watered and salivated thinking about eating that yummy *pyrohy* slathered in sour cream with butter, onions, or mushroom sauce and bacon bits on top.

Oye, she was getting hungry! She might have to go to "Taste of Ukraine" one of her favorite restaurants in Saskatoon on 22nd street to eat. Or maybe the *babas* and *didos*, the grandmothers and grandfathers at the many Ukrainian churches were busy cooking. She knew many volunteers were fundraising for many churches and auditoriums by having an "All You Can Eat" *perogy* supper tonight.

Saskatoon was known as the volunteer capital of Canada as more people per capital volunteer. Saskatchewan is also known as one of the friendliest places in the world. DD considered Saskatoon her home, even though she still loved to go to Hafford to see her *batko* or father, who still lived there among his relatives.

Ukrainians are known for their notorious work ethics and strong faith, family, food, fun and cultural heritage which fashioned DD's drive, determination, and desire to become a daring detective. Where would one find a sharper, wittier and cunning gal? Who appreciated or needed a female with an exceptional clever ability, mind, and talent in such a small place with so little crime? Her future shined in the big city, and what a future she had planned for herself.

Deirdre always desired to be a detective right from the get-go. Her father, Bohdan, which means gift from God, received his Bachelor of Law Degree (LLB) from the University of Saskatchewan in Saskatoon and then through scholarships and hard work went on to complete his Doctorate of Civil Law (D.L.C.) and Juris Doctor from McGill in Montreal, Quebec, Canada.

Once, a high-profile criminal lawyer, he would often discuss interesting cases with her. Although now retired, his expert consultation was continuously available as he advised many famous lawyers via zoom, twitter, text messages and e-mail. Naturally, DD became his soundboard and unknowingly at the time, the means and unofficial training to attain a detective's credentials.

Married late, in Bohdan's career, he left Hafford to go to university. He started a family at the age of 49. His short marriage left him isolated to raise a wonderful, exceptional daughter. At the age of five Deirdre's mother, Sophie, died of cancer. Deirdre's only living relative on her mother's side was a childless, spinster aunt Evelyn. Her mom's sister wanted to take her to live in Regina, Saskatchewan. Her father refused and moved DD to where both her parents grew up and her mom was now buried in Hafford close to her parents, Tessie Woznakowski and Stefan Dubyk.

Retirement and solitude gave them precious time together. Her dad, an avid reader and mentor, incredibly early, enrolled his daughter into the many Mystery Book Clubs while surfing the net. At the tender age of eight, Deirdre, the youngest member of the Mystery Guild Club, was already a prolific reader. She devoured and digested every old or recently written mystery book on the market and at the Hafford Library.

Clever detectives like the Hardy Boys, Trixie Belden, and of course her favorite female detective Nancy Drew intrigued her. At ten, thrilled by Stephen King and consumed by Tom Clancy's espionage and Dean Kootz's suspense, she especially enjoyed reading women writers. Agatha Christie, Mary Higgins Clarke and Sue Grafton and Canadian mystery writers Gail Bowen, Louise Penny and Kathy Reichs were among her favorites with their thrilling books.

Deirdre clearly foresaw the path she was heading in life and so did her father. While her classmates played soccer, experimented with makeup, had sleepovers, giggled, or dated boys; DD was a loner who was solving crimes and developing her future as a daring detective.

13 years later, at 18, a metamorphic miracle occurred, and a beautiful butterfly emerged from her cocoon. Deirdre dropping that dowdy look, now resembled a southern bell hailing not from Georgia or even Alabama; but *tak*, yes Hafford, if one can compare Saskatchewan to the old south.

Quite frankly, my dear Deirdre, upon grade twelve graduation, shed her feathers and flew the coup. Embarking on an incredible journey, besides her wildest dreams; she entered places where this girl had never gone before. Her precise plan unfolded in Saskatoon, a city, with surrounding areas of about 300,000 people.

Deirdre's life changed thanks to Clairol, beauty salons, makeovers, laser surgery, fitness clubs and spin places like the lovely new Life CYCLE Spin Studio on Broadway. With self-help books and significant shopping at all the right places like Michael Kors, The Bay, Sandbox in the City and Whipped Cream she blossomed. Consequently, DD entered the picture as a sophisticated, confident woman sporting a stylish, Ukrainian accent, using it often, as she learned English and Ukrainian at the same time. Her mom had spoken to her in both languages as a baby, so she really had no accent but preferred her mama's roots.

In her younger days, her body was amorphous. But now her figure fully developed due to persistent hard work, joining the gym, spin cycling, taking martial arts, kickboxing, tai chi, handball, yoga as well as routinely running five kilometers in the rain, shine or even snow, near the University Bridge and River Landing area. DD was now described by the Canadian press, The Globe and Mail and the Saskatoon Star Phoenix as "an extremely attractive, unattached lady."

Coveting a glamorous figure from the olden days of 36, 24, 36, she was often referred to as a perfect ten. Her talented hairdresser, Shelly, designed a glossy, raven, and sassy short coiffure. Styled just above her shoulders, the bottom edge curled forward, displaying a sharp contrast to her stunning blue eyes transformed by contacts. Her beauty and charm added flavour to this dish. Her glamour made her one of the most desirable bachelorettes in Saskatoon or even Saskatchewan, perhaps even Canada or *mozhe buty*, maybe even the world.

Yoi! Is it too pretentious to say—oh, let it be known! DD now resembled a raven-haired Greek goddess. Because she was from Saskatchewan and about 13 per-cent of the population were of Ukrainian descent, she therefore resembled a Ukrainian princess, her genetics consisted of those lovely features. Even today, many men travel to Ukraine just to find a wife and marry Ukrainian women as they are recognized as some of the most amazing, beautifully featured women in the world.

DD was admired by many, not just for her looks, but more importantly, she was a successful female role model and was smart as a whip. Beauty and brains, she had it all!

This morning too, would be described as gorgeous in sunny Saskatoon known as the sunshine capital of Canada. DD pulled up to the curb in front of the flower shop below her trendy Broadway office near Five Corners. Her slender fingers delicately twisted the ignition key and extinguished the sound of her powerful engine on her vehicle that was noticeably meant for racing.

A midnight blue, metallic custom paint job matched her eyes. With tucked and rolled white leather seats, DD loved her 64 Le Mans convertible. This car was the original GTO known as the "goat." It was the first muscle car few recognized prior to Mustangs hitting the trail. DD picked this car because of its appearance combined with an outstanding roadside performance. Of course, the "package" was also transformed from former days.

Detailed graphics adorn the lower sides of her car. A subtle progression of stars above the rocker; seven symbolic, silver to bright blue faded in and out. For those car fanatics, DD's mechanic, Volodymyr, who built street rods, took a 389-tri power, which develops tremendous horsepower. Known as a "street sleeper" this car is as good as it gets and can literally outperform most vehicles on the road.

Deciding to capitalize on "DD," she believed the initials on her license plate represented a dramatic transformation from her previous life as "Dowdy Deirdre." DD now stood for "Dazzling Detective."

The image reflected by her sporty number was true to the character that DD enjoys today- stunning. Her transportation truly is a visual representation of her new adult life.

Opening the door on the street side, simply lifting her leg out of her car electrified the air. The two male bystanders were originally ogling the auto, but now were distracted by DD's elicit *krasa*, beauty, grace, and style. With the car door open, twisting her body, DD placed her left foot on the pavement, purposely pausing a moment. Then, before following with her right leg, she exposed her upper thigh totally understanding the noticeable outcome it had on the two men.

Most males on the hunt would start at the top and work down when describing female prey. But with DD—wow, does she have legs. Her best assets are worthy of any large insurance policy. The knobby-kneed girl had blossomed into a long-legged jaguar; a tall, lithe, feisty creature. One must again comment on her tremendous, exceptional, spectacular legs as most eyes are drawn to this feature first.

Framing her bright red, pedicure painted nails, are four-inch spiked open-toed red, patent leather heels. Two straps from the center of the sole of her shoe cross at her ankle. At the back, below her shapely calves, it crosses over once again, then returns to the front. Two diamond shaped clips are perfectly located around the back, above the lower leg muscles. Her muscular calves are quite indicative of someone who performs strenuous athletics.

Some people say she wears her skirts a little short, but they are just prudes. Those people were from Deirdre's former life. In DD's new vitality, skirts wider than belts are quite acceptable because of course, she has the lean thighs to wear those types of clothes. Heads turn, jealous women turn green and understandably the opposite sex drools when DD steps into the scene. Seductively, she elevates herself out of the car.

Immaculately and impeccably attired, she prefers to wear white, a sign of her purity, high class and well suited for business. Today, DD wore a characteristic mini-skirt and white satin top. Standing close by, most would notice her fine firm 36c cleavage accentuated by the extra button undone. Her lacy bra under her see-through blouse is provocative, while remaining sophisticated as well as tasteful. Adjusting her blouse, DD lightly puts her finely manicured, long red fingernails and palms on her slim waist. Very slowly, she pushes them over her elegant hips to smooth her short skirt.

Accenting her graceful, long attractive neckline was a quaint, gold diamond pendant with matching earring studs. A one-carat Canadian diamond ring adorns her right ring finger. This set was given to Deirdre at age 18 by her father. Originally, he had bought it for her mother, for Sophie's wedding day. It is the only item DD kept from her former existence.

She is reminded of her personal life's philosophy and enjoys characteristics common to Ukrainian people. They love to decorate and are proud of their culture. With strong ethics, Ukrainians contribute greatly to making Saskatchewan the wonderful place it is in Canada. Saskatchewan's Former Premier, Brad Wall honoured Ukrainians and their ancestors by declaring 2016 the "Year of Saskatchewan Ukrainians."

DD was proud to attend the wonderful National banquet and gala showcase in the province's capital of Regina, Saskatchewan on September 30th, at the Conexus Arts Centre. What a marvelous event presented by the Ukrainian Canadian Congress and Saskatchewan. It was filled with song, dance, and fun! Saskatoon's own Pavlychenko Folklorique Ensemble performed, "Baba's Trunk" and Lastiwka Ukrainian Orthodox Choir & Orchestra from Saskatoon sang. Also performing and now living in New York, was a fine jazz musician born in Edmonton, Alberta, John Stetch on piano and from Toronto Ron Cahute on accordion. Originally, from Ukraine, but now living in Toronto was Vasyl Popadiuk on violin. Together, they played a fantastic Folk fusion. It was a three-hour showcase explosion of Ukrainian talent and a time to celebrate Ukrainian culture and traditions.

DD's roots distinguish her unique character and appearance from other detectives. "It's the extra, little things you do that matter and make a major difference in your life." She wanted things to be *duzhe dobre*, or very good.

Placing the keys in her petit, over the shoulder, rouge purse, she loved red accessories, DD sways her hip to close the car door. The two fellows watching from the sidewalk nudge each other as they lean to follow her movements. Their eyes rivet to her backside and legs. DD knows all too well the result she has on men.

These two guys don't recognize "Dowdy Deirdre" from their high school days together in Hafford. DD steps to the sidewalk, sensuously smiling. She removes her designer Oakley sunglasses and tosses them on the passenger side of the bucket seat.

Turning, making direct eye contact, she purrs at the men, *"Dobry den,* good day, Mykolai, Vasyl."

Brushing past them, opening the stairway door leading to her office above Tatiana's Flower Shop, they are absolutely stunned. Exactly, the effect she wanted. Slowly, ascending the steps, she knew their eyes would follow her through the door for a second look. Their imaginations working overtime, a large Cheshire cunning smile returns to DD's face.

Chapter 3

RAUNCHY

Near the top of the stairs, hearing the familiar Latin flavored tempo of music pervading from behind the office door, DD anticipates the scene waiting. She opens the door. Raunchy, feet crossed on his desk, leans way back in the black leather recliner, a position most would use for sleeping. Not Raunchy. Although, looking a little hung over from last night's escapades, he holds his cellphone and file folder tightly in his hands.

A basic functional office, recent discussion entailed around the acquisition of a new premise. The need to hire an assistant at their agency was urgent. Clientele and status skyrocketed these past three years from all their successful cases and their reputation was growing daily.

Raunchy's desk was located on the right side of the door. DD's cherry oak, antique bureau was on his right and faced the front door. Several degrees and a classic photograph, taken by the late local artist Courtney Milne of the Bessborough Hotel at night, framed the walls, as well as a print by the late Ukrainian artist, William Kurelek. The standard matching cherry wood file cabinet in the corner separated their space. A large, exotic orchard changed the business-like atmosphere. Two, black leather recliners with a bamboo magazine rack was behind a full wall mural left of the door.

The mural painted by Raunchy resembled an English scene from a spy novel. Complete with London fog encompassing a dim streetlight there was a man in a black trench coat, face hidden by his upturned collar. Having little difficulty agreeing on interior design, "the partners in crime" had such similar tastes that it was sometimes spooky.

DD respectfully had office reminders of her roots, with a pot of sunflowers in the corner and on her desk behind a glass case was an exquisite *pysanka* or decorated Easter egg written by Saskatoon renowned artist, Gerry Zerbecky. The symbols written on the egg reminded her of her great-grandmother, red poppies for her homeland of Ukraine and yellow wheat for their farming ancestral background and blue to match the wide prairie sky.

Raunchy, her associate, dons the tightest blue jeans you have ever seen except of course, when wearing his black designer jeans. Rumour has it that when they met, both were clad with body skimming, virtually identical apparel. Apparently, DD tracked Raunchy to the infamous Studio 54 Disco Club. Raunchy sporting clinging white pants, a flashy, red belt and a white shirt unbuttoned to the navel, wore precisely the same outfit as DD.

They spent the weekend together exploring the beautiful sights of New York, attended a Broadway musical called "Les Misérables" and even had time to visit the east village and lower east side called Manhattan's *borsch* belt. Nothing feels as good as eating a hot bowl of *borsch*, Ukrainian beet soup, rye bread and *kovbasa* with a side dish of *perogies*.

Raunchy was hooked with this interesting foreign diet. DD promised to take him back to experience the restaurant, "*Veselka*" which serves a traditional Ukrainian twelve meatless dishes, a dinner called "*Sviat Vechir*." This important spiritual meal for Ukrainians is eaten before Liturgy on January sixth to celebrate Ukrainian Christmas Eve.

Instantly, setting eyes on DD, believing his destiny was fulfilled, Raunchy's heart flipped, besought by his soul mate. Always number one in life and on top of everything, Raunchy dove into their relationship. He tried to harangue and carry off the love of his life. His supposed newest flame, DD, was quietly amused at this seductive venture. She viewed him as a great source of fun and entertainment. DD was all business; hence she had other intentions for him.

After their initial meeting in New York three years earlier, DD detected a great sleuth in Raunchy. Dismissing his courtship, she immediately works to import him from the States. Raunchy, thinking pursuit of quest, was still hoping to obtain the elusive, evasive notch on his pistol handle. However, DD, the expert fisherwoman set the bait, hauled him in, and lured him to Saskatchewan. DD knows what she wants and "always gets her man." To this day, she is still one up on Raunchy.

But all this is perhaps, only rumour speaking. In Raunchy's world he is known as a true Hound Dog. (Not the Presley kind) Sniffing out clues, he rapidly achieved results. Together, DD and Raunchy make an impressive pair. A true working couple, trying to create a safer, more peaceful, and better world.

Raunchy, a teenage playboy handle he kept was named Raoul Sanchero Rodriguez Chiaz Santiago. He was born and raised in New York City. Of course, he was always the tough character with dark skin and brown eyes. A definite charmer, his suave, debonair attitude makes him a real lady's man despite his 172.5 centimeters stature - tall for a Mexican. Women adore him and his accent only assists with wooing the opposite sex. When he speaks of *amour* or love in Spanish, women go completely wild.

Raunchy's jet-black hair was always tightly pulled back in a ponytail. Presenting an image of a shrewd, classic Latino look, he resembled a younger Antonio Banderas. His smile flashed one gold plated tooth which radiates perfect sparkling white teeth without the assistance of childhood braces.

His sleek, Italian leather shoes, designer jeans, black Mexican belt were decorated with silver conchos. Silk multi-coloured shirts, a long, gold chain and a gold #1 imprinted a large, diamond piercing in his left ear. He resonated an image of a Mexican lover. The row of gold, shiny rings on his left hand highlighted a Rolex watch. When turning his forearm, a beautiful coloured, bold tattoo of a Hound Dog with its nose sniffing to the ground is visible. Ladies viewed him as the perfect ten too.

His vehicle enables rapid travel in his speed filled life. A shiny, red 71 Monte Carlo SS, a low rider was customized with hydraulics. The low-profile car was customized with 18-inch gold spinner wheels, the interior decorated with blue dingle balls and fuzzy purple dice. The car had air bags that lowered to four inches off the ground when parked. This spicy looking machine carries a license plate, "Snoop 1," announcing to the universe his self-proclaimed image as Hot Tamale, Top Dog, Spicy Mexican and Magnificent Lover.

Not your average person. Elevate your thoughts to a well-groomed classy Mexicano or Chicano. The tantalizing scent of Don Juan said *amante*. Raunchy openly declares his conquests proudly. Alas, *carino* or love is not always fair when it comes to the affairs of the heart. Raunchy openly laments for DD daily.

"I've got it." DD announced and beamed with a wide grin, ear to ear. Singing victoriously, ei, ei, ei, oh during her moments of triumph, she melodically swings open the door.

Raunchy's mind was racing. Here, before his eyes was still the most desirable exploration. Unable to capture her heart, he knew he would never give up on her. He would continuously bid for her love with the greatest motivation and passion.

"Raunchy, I need you to run out to Kenaston, Saskatchewan and check something in a garage."

Kenaston, was a farming village, known for the Super Draft hockey fundraiser held annually, a place of about 285 people. It is located 55 minutes from Saskatoon, an easy drive on the divided highway about 82 kilometers away passing through Dundurn, and Hanley, Saskatchewan.

The Ukrainian/Slavic author that wrote the award winning, national bestselling Baba's Babushka books grew up there. In winter, some people become storm stayed in that village. The wind howls and the snow blows fiercely at times, making Kenaston the blizzard capital of Saskatchewan. Tourists are attracted to their gigantic, symbolic snowman downtown.

Setting the file folder on his desk, Raunchy brings his chair to an upright position ready for action. His eyes devour the radiant look of his partner. Hopefully very soon, she would be his gal. Standing before him while seductively dressed in white, his mind flashes back to their first meeting. His desire for her was always the primary focus of his attention.

"Sure boss, what am I looking for?" He flashes his best sexy smile. "Sounds like you found a solution to our dilemma."

"I believe we just need to wrap up the evidence, then crucify." DD was relaxed. Solving the case enabled her to be problem free and refreshed. She would be able to collect some zzz's later today.

Chapter 4

THE COUPLE

How does one describe Dwayne? How does one describe Marianne? As a couple, they are like two peas in a pod or ketchup and fries. Childhood sweethearts, dating since age 12, they were always together. But of course, in elementary school, Dwayne would pull Marianne's pigtails. Then as they grew older, he would chase her and later try and steal kisses when no one was looking.

Being such a big tease, Marianne would let him catch her. When playing tag, she would coax him to kiss her. She was clearly in control, allowing Dwayne's dominance whenever it suited her. As time progressed, it was inevitable their marriage would occur young. Dwayne loved wearing Marianne on his arm as his showpiece. She was his arm candy. Dwayne lusted for Marianne and she deeply enjoyed the attention he expressed as affection.

Dwayne was a typical, small town guy, running a small-town garage, in a small town. Car problems call Dwayne on his cell at 223-6837 or 2be-Over. His advertising jingle-jangle rang out a cute jingle, "Want your car problems 2be over? One call and they're over. Call me at 2be-over! That's 223-6837."

Marianne was a small-town girl, cute with blue eyes, blonde hair, and a svelte figure other women envy. Men were attracted to her bubbly personality. Her polite soft-spoken voice and demeanor suited her extra-long, French pearl white, manicured, gel nails. A mechanic's dream in a class of her own, she had all the right parts, in all the right places. Dwayne being "the mechanic" could handle her curves as a daytime, nighttime or anytime driver.

Marianne spent her days running from clothing stores to the beauty parlor, two favorite places she frequented. She loved spending money and looking pretty, sometimes more than she loved Dwayne. 18 years of so-called wedded bliss and at the age of 36, Marianne was a well-preserved Diva.

A doublewide trailer with an attached auto garage was where Dwayne worked on his cars. A trailer court on the outskirts of Kenaston was their abode. Dwayne enjoyed having the guys over for a few beers, especially on Friday nights after work. They played a little poker, smoked a couple of cigars, relaxed and told off-colour jokes.

Playing the perfect hostess, Marianne would flirt and charm the guys with her small talk. Of course, the guys loved her attractive female scenery. Dwayne took great pride in having the guys look at his property, for it elevated his ego and his position in town. Well known as being his decorated hood ornament, Marianne was helpful at times and awfully good for the beer run and chips. This set up, happily suited them both and they seemed to have the "perfect marriage."

However, there was one tiny, little sore spot in their marriage that irritated Marianne. At times, Dwayne could be awfully tight fisted with his money. He would never spend money needlessly, especially on cars. An excellent mechanic with 20 years of experience, he refused to buy Marianne a new car.

"I can fix it." Dwayne would slur. "It is still chugging."

Marianne still had the first car her daddy bought her at the age of 16. An original 68 Monaco, white, four-door sedan with a six cylinder.

"Sure," Dwayne stated, "It ain't the perfect car, but it's sensible, reliable and cheap on gas."

It was even rust free in most parts, with only a small dent in the backdoor, a tiny scar in the life of a Monaco. Lately, it seemed her "reliable" car was becoming rather "unreliable." Marianne hassled Dwayne for a new car.

"Why can't I get a new car? Do you realize that one day, I am going to be late for my hair appointment?" whined Marianne on a regular basis.

Complaints Dwayne ignored.

"Have you any idea how hard it is to get into Nancy as she is so overbooked? I can't go out in public without my hair done," she pouted.

"Honey," Dwayne would relate, "Call me anytime for you know my jingle, sweetie. Car troubles. Just call me 2be-over. That's 2BE-OVER. 223-6837 and I'll always come and get you, sugar."

Dwayne loved that cute jingle and sang it more often than it appeared on the radio.

Marianne was ticked at Dwayne. Her car problems made her blood boil. She began experiencing nightmares. She dreamt she was stranded all alone in the desert without water, thirsty or stuck on the highway in the pouring rain. No help, her hair ruined and her clothes filthy. She had even broken a nail in one of her dreams. Sometimes, she even dreamed about death.

At wit's end, she went to see Dr. Knowes, her physician. She told him about her bad dreams and sleeping anxiety. The doctor, completely understanding the workings of women, prescribed sleeping pills for nighttime relief and Prozac to settle her nerves during the day.

"You're working too hard," he chirped. "Go and get yourself a new outfit. You deserve it and you'll feel a lot better. And make sure you book an appointment to visit me each week."

He too, smitten by her beauty, enjoyed the distraction and attraction she offered from his daily routine of patients that were sick. Dr. Knowe's office was located above Slim Hope's Insurance shop. That is where Marianne got the idea to get insurance. Car breakdowns and dreams about death were all a bad sign. She decided to pop into the insurance office downstairs to see what was cooking.

Luckily, the owner, Slim, the nice insurance man completely understood her problem. He suggested the two for one special. Having vented her problems to Slim, it made Marianne immediately feel better. She thought Dwayne would go for it, as he loved to save money and was always looking for a cheap deal.

Slim married June Hope ten years ago. On his wedding day, he inherited his father's insurance business as a present from his father, Mo Payne. The enterprise, however, was on the verge of bankruptcy. Rather than change the name of the company to Slim Payne, being extremely superstitious, he felt there was little chance he would succeed at an establishment with that name. His father barely survived this lucrative industry during his lifetime.

It's believed that an apple never falls far from the tree. But Slim was seemingly brighter than his dad. He knew that expression and understood it. No desire to follow in his papa's footsteps, breaking with tradition, he legally changed his last name to his wife's name. That is how he became Slim Hope, deciding that this name would bring profit to his venture.

Customers being unsuspectingly hopeful when buying insurance, perceived they might receive their insurance claims. Slim was clever enough to think he outsmarted his customers. He believed the opposite to be true. Underneath he was a bit of a miser. He unwittingly knew there was "no way in hell" he was ever going to pay out a claim. Unless of course, he was absolutely forced to by law.

Dressed today in his usual purple and grey, plaid fortrel leisure suit and white shoes, Slim had once considered dying his platform shoes. Luckily, he didn't however, as white is always fashionable and matches anything. A prodigy of the 70's, he still walks the talk and plays the part, believing all women adore him. His office is a blast from the past containing a leather duvet and a paisley covered chair. An infamous lavender lava lamp completes the burgundy, shag carpet and psychedelic posters.

Besides his casual flings, golf was another favorite passion. Slim often scored an eagle or three under par, although he had continuous streaks as a bogey golfer. On his walls prominently displayed were autographed photos of three golf masters, Arnold Palmer, Chi Chi Rodriguez, and Ben Hogan taken of course with Slim in a plaid, fortrel suit.

Walking into Slim's office that opportune day, Marianne paused in the doorway to enjoy the glorious sun behind her. The reflection disrobed her as the shimmering sunlight gave Slim an incredible view of a slightly clothed, attractive, female specimen. Realizing this, Marianne stood quietly in the doorway for a few moments to attract attention.

Slim's active hormones accelerated. It was such a slow afternoon. He thought to himself, "a sucker born every minute, got to make a sale, a two for one delight, a gal in the backroom and an extra-large insurance policy."

Standing to greet his next victim, Slim scanned her with lecherous eyes. He knew from previous experience the fastest way to success was to cut to the chase. He tries to throw them off guard with a direct question, yet discreetly proceeds with caution.

With a wry grin, Slim reached for her hand. Immediately placing a little peck curtly on her fingertips, he said, "Your wish is my desire, ma'am." Clearing his throat, trying not to look too obvious and faking a cough, he repeats clearly, "What can I do for you, ma'am?"

Marianne enjoyed the playful approach and lavish attention, responding meaningfully with a silky voice laden with flirtatious intentions, "Anything special available, today?"

He knew his two for one ploy would quickly be fulfilled. Yet, not wanting to rush the afternoon delight, he proceeded confidently, "What exactly do you have in mind? I have many super, extra-large deals to offer, especially to such an attractive woman like yourself."

"Perhaps you should show me."

Gesturing his left hand like a royal attendant, while graciously motioning to the back of the office with his right, he regally beckons to Marianne.

"Please come into my private, back office so we can discuss the exact terms of our agreement more carefully. We can both be more comfortable there. I am positive all your needs will be met with the utmost care and you will completely enjoy the outcome of our arrangement."

"Yes, I agree. A more private discussion is exactly what we need," she purrs. Shifting her body to show off her curves at the best angle, it makes Slim anticipate their discussion.

"Right this way." He followed the blonde beauty.

"Care for a drink?" Slim asks as they sneakily slide off behind the green, beaded curtain.

"Love one, thanks."

Grinning like a lustful fool, Slim flips on his eight track to the sweet sound of *"Love is in the Air."*

Chapter 5

THE DISCUSSION

"What?" Dwayne questioned Marianne later that evening at supper.

"We don't need insurance. I'm never sick and you always look terrific. Why do we need insurance?"

"Soon you'll be 40 honey, you're getting older. What if something happens to your health?"

Fluttering her long, dark, false eyelashes, she reaches across the table. Marianne proceeds to stroke the back of his hand.

"What if something happens in your shop, all alone? Fixing cars is dangerous." Crooning she adds, "Who will support me?"

Since Dwayne is not convinced, she takes it to the next level. Weeping hysterically, Marianne puts her head down on her hands on the table. Those vivid dreams about death had left her in a crazy, frenzied state.

"Besides, everyone has insurance." Marianne complains, "And this is a two for one special being offered just for me... I mean us this week, a onetime chance to get two policies with full benefits for any kind of illness, any accidents or disabilities and a double indemnity payout for an accidental death."

"A special, huh?"

"Yes, just for us. Slim says if we pay the entire year in advance it will only be $1200.00. And Dwaynie, you know I will sleep better if we get this insurance. Then I will be much happier and when I am feeling happy," she suggests, "you know I can make you feel better all over, in oh, so many ways."

Marianne gets up and puts her arms around Dwayne's shoulders, starting to rub his neck. She feels him loosen up a bit. Swaying, relaxing, he thinks about the offer until she opens her mouth and mentions her car. If only she had not brought up the fact that her car breaks down all the time.

That's the real reason she wants insurance, or else he needs to buy her a new car. Nobody makes demands or black mails Dwayne. That blew it. Almost persuaded, Dwayne digs his heels in further. The obstinate, cheap fellow that he really is sticks to his guns. He feels personally violated by her car comment.

Doesn't she realize by now he could fix any vehicle on the road? How many times does he have to tell her that or show her how good he is as a mechanic?

"No insurance, no new car!" he explodes. "Damn it anyway, Marianne. I don't care if it's a two for one special to China. $100.00 a month is $100.00 a month that we do not need to spend. Think about the extra beer and cigars I could buy with that money."

Big tears come to her eyes. Trying to make amends for his explosion and not wanting to sleep on the couch tonight, he adds squeamishly, "Marianne think about the additional outfits you could purchase each month," implies Dwayne. Clothes were always a soft spot with Marianne, it seemed that discussion was over. She left the table and took her unfinished supper plate to the kitchen sink.

That same night was poker night. Joe, Mike, Bruno, Tim, and Dwayne were each sipping back a couple of brews as the bluish cigar smoke filled the trailer. Marianne was alone in the living room writing in her diary when Bruno commented to Dwayne, "Did you have a fight with the missus? She's not teasing us tonight. I miss her sense of humour and good looks."

"Not really a fight." Dwayne snarled at his nosy friends. "She's pissed at me for not buying her a new car, and she wants life insurance, too."

"Shit, is that all," interjected Mike. "Let's all throw a couple hands of poker here so Dwayne can afford the car. I miss her big distractions when I play poker."

"It's always great having her pass me a beer," says Tim putting in his two cents worth.

"If she ain't passing me beer, I don't get no attention or contact from any ladies at all. You're so lucky to have her all to yourself, Dwayne."

Joe starts to grin, not saying a thing. He has been extremely close to Marianne a couple of times previously and knows others have too. Rather curious though, he wonders what was up. It was highly unusual for her to behave antisocial and ignore them this way. He felt uneasy. Something was brewing as Marianne was not completely herself tonight. Neither was Dwayne for that matter. Realizing the situation affecting his good friend and all of them, he decides to change the subject.

"Hey buddy, I sure could use another beer, how about you?"

Dwayne tipped his beer can and drained it.

"Sure thing. Grab us all one but leave Tim alone as he is being celibate. Hard to say the reaction you might get from him."

"Sounds like he's pretty hard up or wants to be," chuckled Bruno.

"Just about out 'a beer," claimed Joe as he returned to the table.

Purposely, putting one hand around each side of Tim, he sets down the can. Then proceeds to rub his chest on the back of Tim's bald head as they all snicker.

Marianne is enticed by the boys' laughter and looks up. She missed their interaction and especially their attention. Seductively, loosening a button on her blouse, adjusting her skirt a little higher, she shakes her hair from side to side entering the poker table area.

"Hey guys," she coos, "miss me?" She raises her eyebrows.

"Joe covered for you," interjected Tim as they laugh loudly again.

"Hey sugar pie, we're low on beer?" Dwayne comments quietly.

For some reason, the hair on the back of her neck twinges.

"NO NEW CAR, NO INSURANCE, NO BEER," she remembers, glaring at her husband. Then she snarls at him, "Just what do you think, that I am supposed to walk to get you that beer?"

Sensing the nervous tension, the men slither snake-like further down into their chairs.

Joe tries to save the moment and speaks first, "Take my truck."

"Thanks Joe."

She turns placing a great, long, wet, kiss on his cheek.

"OK, if I pay you back another day?" she says sweetly, taking the keys and waltzes out the front door. The poker players were embarrassed, lowered their heads and viewed their cards. As they have a sip of beer, they are noticeably quiet, afraid to speak, or make eye contact. A tinge of red rises from their necks.

"How's about we call it a night?" says Dwayne sheepishly.

"Good thing I live close by," says Joe. "I guess I'm walking home. I'll pick up my truck in the morning."

Chapter 6

THE NEXT DAY

The very next morning, while driving to her hair appointment, Marianne re-experiences her nightmare about being stranded on the side of the road. She mentally rehashed last night's dinner conversation when…

Blaam! Her car suddenly jerks to the left and her heart raced. Struggling with the steering wheel, the big, old Monaco catches the soft shoulder of the pavement. Dust flying, tires screeching, she heads for the ditch. Pure luck, not skill, brought the old Dodge to a halt directly in front of a water- filled ravine. Shaking with fear, Marianne tightly grasps the wheel of her car. A blown tire. Great. The knuckles on her hands were white as she regained her thoughts. Aware that she is lucky and grateful to be alive, breathing rapidly, her blood boiled. The putrid smell of fine dust filled the air and her nostrils. Unhurt, but overwrought and now fuming mad, she rummages for her cell phone in her purse.

Cursing as that stupid jingle ran throughout her head.

"Over… call over… to be over."

She recalls Dwayne's silly, smiling, singing face and again remembers his last night's refusal to buy her a new car. The fool. He needed to pay. She was ready to kill him. Now she would miss her bloody hair appointment.

When her ignorant husband answered, Marianne blasted Dwayne on the phone screaming unlike anything she had ever done in their 18 years of marriage. Verbally attacking him on his cell, she insults his intelligence in rude curses while explaining about the blown tire and wreck.

He listens, letting her scream at him. Finally, finished blowing off steam she firmly proclaims, "You better get here right now, and you had better not hang up on me or else. I am not through with you, yet."

Marianne was in a complete state of shock. It did not improve when her husband arrived, in fact, seeing him only increased her anger. Raving mad, she swears and screams at him while Dwayne changes the tire on her Monaco. Nothing she does or says seems to have any effect on her husband. He just keeps changing the tire.

"Do you hear me?"

"Half the planet can hear you, Marianne."

That makes her even angrier. Proceeding to the rear of the car she picks up a rock and chucks it at Dwayne to demonstrate her fury. Seeing the pebble coming, he knows her aim is terrible. He does not have to move and smiles at her. The smirk is what did it.

He should not have smiled. That pissed Marianne off even more. "You rotten son of a bitch," she exclaims, running toward him. Fists flying, with clenched teeth she screams in his ear, "I want a new car. Now!"

Turning, she suddenly kicks over the jack. The car falls on Dwayne. You could hear the cracking of bone as the car lands heavily on her husband's left leg.

"Marianne!"

Seeing Dwayne yelping in agony, Marianne feels a little cooler now. Strangely, her anger has subsided, seemingly displaced with slight pleasure. He yells and this time she gets to ignore him. That feels good.

Smiling to herself, she contemplates getting into Dwayne's tow truck. She feels like leaving him stranded on the side of the road with her old Monaco resting on his crushed leg and driving away forever. Immoral, illegal thoughts surface, as a huge, volcanic eruption occurs inside her mind.

What was happening to her?

Where were these horrific ideas coming from?

She never imagined she could think or feel this way.

"Maybe I should finish him off," she mutters to herself, watching him yell for help, reaching to grab the fallen jack, working it enough to wiggle out from beneath the edge of the fallen car.

His cries stir vengeful, murderous thoughts. Marianne stands watching, letting him save himself. Letting Dwayne believe she was too shocked to respond, too helpless to assist her husband, he does not question her cool reaction.

Inside, Marianne's mind is racing.

"No, not now, I need insurance first. Get the insurance and then... my new car, any car." Imagining herself driving down the highway in a sleek, red mustang convertible, the sun shining on her face she suddenly felt ecstatic. The pressure released; she feels better.

Calling 911, while waiting for the ambulance to come, she pretended to be concerned, oblivious to Dwayne's whimpering.

Marianne started to entertain a plan. She needs to find some way to **off** her husband. A murder, not just an ordinary death, but an accident. That's it, a logical, accidental incident. What she needed was a **Perfect Murder**. Planned, calculated, and executed to perfection.

Amazed at her calm nature and complete logic, Marianne was surprised that she was having these thoughts now. Thinking, yes, she was thinking for herself. She was considering, devising events she never believed herself capable of creating or deliberating, let alone implementing. And she felt totally at peace planning it.

As the first responders checked and stabilized Dwayne's leg while lifting him on the stretcher, Marianne was aware that she was a different person. Not herself anymore, but a better, stronger, revised, improved, more modern Marianne had come to life. Totally confident, she finally realized she could have whatever she craved. For the first time in 18 years, she was thinking for herself.

Suddenly, comprehending the eminent situation, Marianne concluded that she would never have to rely on a man entirely again to make her wishes and heart's aspirations come true. Riding along with Dwayne to the hospital, she felt it did not matter when Dwayne stated sweetly, "Don't worry darling, I'll have your car running in a jiffy, just as soon as they set my cast. I'll be good as new shortly and ready to have your car rolling, so you can be rocking." Dwayne recanted.

The blaring sirens seemed to mesmerize Marianne and she whispered, "Sure, sure, sure, honey whatever you say. It will be all over soon, real soon," she smiled to herself. She knew it didn't matter what he said anymore.

Chapter 7

JOE

Dwayne, stuck hobbling around with a leg cast, made him a much easier person to persuade to buy life insurance, even authorizing the complete two for one package.

Marianne was still extremely flustered by the whole affair, especially since she missed her weekly hair appointment that critical day. She easily convinced Dwayne to take out the double indemnity accidental death benefits also.

It was a good deal. Slim said so. They signed the check, and everyone smiled. Much more relaxed and heavily insured, Marianne was easier to get along with and she stopped talking about buying a new car. Her sleeping problems and bad dreams disappeared. Dwayne too, felt better. As promised, he had her car up and ready to go as soon as he was released from the hospital.

Two days later, the mechanic was out in the garage working on his poker buddy, Joe's car, and hobbling around with a broken leg to boot. Nothing could keep Dwayne from his passion. Joe laughed aloud when Dwayne re-told the significant events leading to his cracked appendage and all the extra insurance he took out because of the accident.

"Maybe," suggested Joe, "the wife's planning to knock you off now that you have all that extra insurance."

"Yeah, sure," Dwayne chuckled. "Or me her, as it was a two for one special."

Joe sounding startled says, "I ain't never heard of a two for one special for insurance. Maybe hamburgers and Happy Hour drinks or movies, but not insurance."

"Well," Dwayne says, "It's an anniversary special. Apparently, the owner, Slim Payne, I mean Hope is celebrating his 25th anniversary of selling insurance."

"Naw, come off it," honks Joe. "That Slim's so stingy. He would never give anything away for free. I've known him and his wife for years. He's a real miser when it comes to the old pocketbook and his wife's not much to look at either, a bit gone in the head if you ask me."

"Well, it wasn't me who crafted the deal. My wife, Marianne, she got the bargain. The whole enchilada too, for the both of us. It's a real steal."

"I bet," smirked Joe, knowing what a tease Marianne was as their neighbor.

Frequently, he enjoyed many sneak peeks at Dwayne's partially clothed, sunbathing wife. Perhaps, thought Joe, the missus was selling something else. The neighbor smiled to himself knowing both Marianne and Slim. His imagination working overtime, he knew all too well what "special" Slim would offer up. Not wanting Dwayne to be upset and worry about his wayward wife since the mechanic might not finish fixing his car, Joe kept his mouth shut.

"Lucky bugger you are, to get that good policy. I suppose you're worth more dead than alive?" Joe spouted, laughing at the irony that was oblivious to the hardworking mechanic.

"Aren't we all," chuckled Dwayne. "Aren't we all."

But at lunchtime, Dwayne began to think about his relationship with Marianne. While eating his burrito, he seemed to get a bad case of heartburn that started in his throat and continued down into his stomach. He kept hearing his neighbor Joe, laughing.

Their conversation replayed like a movie inside his head. Dwayne could feel tightness in his throat he had never experienced. Feeling uneasy, he suddenly remembered picking up a car last week at a rest stop. He had noticed his wife's Monaco there. Wondering what she was doing out there, he later questioned her about the incident that night.

Sighing, she said softly, "Sugar pie, I was going for a walk on the outdoor paths. I joined a walking group and we are trying to get in touch with nature."

That day, he believed her. Tired from that day's work and his leg aching, he easily accepted her answer. He had been in such a rush to fix Tim's car that day, as he needed to go to Saskatoon and back to get parts. He really had paid no attention to their conversation.

Today, he really wondered if he had missed something. Thinking back now, he began to question her answers from that day. Curiously aware, he knew that Marianne was not a nature lover. The outdoor weather wasn't kind, the bugs often interfered with her hair or messed up her outfits. Heaven forbid! She might even break a nail.

"What was she really doing out there that day?" He wondered, suspiciously.

He tried to envision the other vehicles in the parking lot that day. His mind focused on a white, tacky van. "Whose van was that? Did it have a name on it? A company van perhaps?" He wondered aloud.

Racking his brain, Dwayne tried to remember the name on that van. He couldn't recall it. Perhaps it would come to him later. Still experiencing slight heartburn from his lunch, something else was beginning to evolve and brew in his chest. Doubt and suspicion stirred.

Was he becoming paranoid? He felt he had women's intuition about something, knowing something was wrong. But how could such a man's man like himself, have women's intuition? It was silly. Or was it? Then Dwayne recalled Marianne's conversation with Mr. Hope on the phone the other night. Visualizing her movements as she spoke, he pictured their conversation.

"Mr. Hope, this is Marianne. Remember me, the one you offered that special two for one deal?"

Twisting their antique phone cord around her forefinger, she crossed her legs and tapped her foot on the floor. She seemed to sway to imaginary music. Listening for a moment while Slim spoke, she moaned several times and smiled.

"Of course, I would," she had agreed.

Again, she listened to the insurance salesman, nodding her head to everything he said. That smile stayed on her lips.

"Great," she responded. "I'll be there."

As she hung up the phone, appearing to be in her own little world, she had twirled and danced around like a teenager. Then she had laughed aloud, catching him watching.

"What's up, Marianne?"

"Oh nothing," she giggled.

Was she embarrassed or maybe nervous?

Dwayne watched her from across the room totally confused by her actions. Hearing the conversation, knowing she agreed to an appointment, he innocently quizzed, "When are you going to get it?"

Marianne's pretty face flushed pink as she blushed noticeably, not answering right away, looking at him as if she couldn't find the right words. Again, Dwayne stated, "When are you going for the special? The two for one deal?"

Struggling to answer, Marianne turned toward the washroom to hide her fluster and rambles, "Oh soon, in an hour or so."

"Isn't it a little late for today?" Dwayne added very dismayed. It was already 8:00 p.m.

"Mr. Hope is on call 24 hours of the day like you, honey. Business is business, all the time."

"Ok," Dwayne agreed. It made sense. Then suggested because he was bored, "I am not working too much now with this damn cast. I'll come with you."

"Oh no, I can handle it," she blurted out. Then she had appeared nervous, shifting her legs while skimming both hands down her clothes.

"Sweetums, you rest, no need to drag your leg down there. Remember, the doctor said you are to put your leg up." She called to him from the bathroom. "I'll finish the deal quickly and bring the papers back for you to sign."

"Are you sure?"

Peering around the corner at him, she purred like a sweet kitten, "I want to look after my poor baby, when he's hurt."

"Alright," Dwayne had agreed, enjoying the sensual tease. When she acted like that, it always boosted his ego. "I trust you can handle that huge deal."

Marianne licked her red lipstick covered lips, giving him a sexy smile. "Oh yeah, I know what to do. You've taught me well, Dwaynie. I can handle anything now."

Remembering the scenario that night, Dwayne knew today, that something wasn't adding up. There were too many coincidences. He was not being paranoid. Something was amiss.

A small-town boy cannot be fooled, not Dwayne. He vowed to find out what was going on. What were Joe's remarks concerning his wife? Who was this Slim Hope guy, anyway?

"I know," he says smartly. "I'll find her diary and check out what's really going on in her spinney mind. She writes everything down daily, in that crummy, little book."

Dwayne easily located Marianne's chronicle that had been left on her nightstand. Stretching back on their bed he peruses the pages. It read like a Kardashian reality TV show. The situation that unfolds, as he reads her words written about her life with him stuns and hurts. He finds he can hardly control his seeping, underlying anger while scanning the passages in her journal.

Struggling to comprehend her secret hatred and wish to be free of him, Dwayne can barely fathom how the love of his life can construct such a vicious scheme against him. The conniving plot conceived by his wife was impressive. Her cunning ability to deviously design such a complicated strategic maneuver held him in awe.

"What was **really** going on in her mind?" He wondered flabbergasted.

Did he really know his wife after 18 years together? How could his childhood sweetheart devise such a nasty, plan against him, the love of her life?

What was he to do with this unnerving discovery?

Should he confront her, show her his findings?

He pondered the thought of writing her a disclosure letter in her journal. No, not that. Something else. His thoughts had never been so cluttered and confused in his entire life. He felt the ultimate betrayal pitted in his stomach and was suddenly, saddened by the whole affair.

What would be the result of her deception?

Where would this lead? He felt duped.

Is she playing him for the fool? Never would he dream she could outwit him.

"So, that's why she wanted all that money for buying insurance."

For the first time in Dwayne's entire married life to Marianne, he had a hateful feeling of disloyalty. His world was crumbling down all around him.

Chapter 8

ANOTHER BREAKDOWN

Her vehicle stalled again. Marianne was completely fed up with Mr. Dwayne, I'll Fix Anything and her Monaco. She decides to hitch a ride to town with a friendly, handsome, young man in his shiny, silver BMW convertible. At least that was entertaining.

"Soon," she contemplates, "I will be cruising town in one of these beauties."

Leaving her husband an amusing message on his answering machine, she tries not to sound too cheery as she informs him.

"The beast deserted me again, so it's yours for the taking."

Marianne laughs rather hysterically to herself. The conception of her conspiracy was coming to fruition. Her abandonment of her car was the beginning of the end. Scheming, she recalls her plans. When Dwayne comes to pick up the car, he'll get his own medicine back. She rigged the brakes on his tow truck.

Anticipating news of an imminent crash, it was eerie to hear Dwayne's voice on her cell a while later as she sat in the salon and enjoyed her manicure from her special esthetician, Margaret.

"I can't come get your car," he coldly informed. "The brakes on the tow truck are acting up. You will have to wait."

She hung up fuming after he claimed to be too busy to tend to her needs and instructed Marianne to catch a ride home from a friend.

"Darn, how did he discover that brake problem so swiftly? Has he caught on to her?" Marianne wondered.

Dwayne had foiled her plan. Immediately, she commenced the workings of another rendezvous with death. She needed to act fast now to not arouse her hubby's suspicion.

Dwayne really had to do some talking to get Marianne to help him retrieve her car she left on the side of the road. He borrowed his neighbour Joe's rig as his tow truck was on the fritz, the brakes still not working properly. It was a vigorous job operating the small, cable winch to load the Monaco onto the flatbed. The ramps on Joe's trailer were not stable and belonged to another unit. They did not attach properly to the rear and were sliding around, causing him constant grief.

"If I wasn't so cheap, I would leave this wreck in the ditch," Dwayne speculated. "But I can get a couple hundred bucks from someone restoring one of these old relics."

He had almost come to terms with the idea of a new car for his beloved. However, after his recent discovery and her plot to kill him, that was out of the question.

Marianne had been such a bear lately; she did not seem to care anymore. Acting strangely, she argued and expressed her opinions often.

"Great, a thinking wife, just what I need, another huge headache."

Loading the behemoth, hunk of metal, Marianne verbally abused him again. When would she shut up? Non-stop complaints. She's acting like other women.

"Doesn't she get it? I am still the best mechanic for miles around and she is just The Mechanic's Wife. I can fix anything." Dwayne was exceptionally annoyed today.

The mental anguish from his wife's deceit was showing, compounded by the heat. It was extremely hot day, 30 degrees Celsius. The sun was sweltering down. His broken leg ached from all the physical strain. Biting his tongue, he decided not to say a word about his discovery from her diary to her yet. Keep the peace for now.

"She keeps going on about her car, the more she rants and raves the stronger I feel about fixing her," he mumbled to himself. "She is really getting to me, her constant nagging, going ta hafta show 'er whose boss," he says under his breath as he started to tie down her car.

"Marianne, you need to help me unload your car into my shop?" Dwayne demands when they get home.

"I can't help. I just got my nails done," exclaimed Marianne.

"It won't require using your hands, except on the steering wheel of the car and your feet on the brakes. I need someone to work the brake while I unload our car. I can't do it alone."

Reluctantly, she agreed.

"You need to continually apply the brake." Dwayne explains loudly in an insistent voice, concerned Marianne was not taking the unloading seriously enough.

"That is the most important thing," his voice was quite demeaning, making his point. "When we back the car down, keep your foot lightly on the brake, at all times. These ramps I borrowed from Joe are unstable and may slip."

Dwayne wondered if he should have gotten one of the guys to help. He had little faith in women drivers, let alone his wife and her perfect plan. Moving the vehicle required enough momentum to get onto the ramps, yet not too much or it would push the car off the ramps.

"You must slowly apply brake pressure. Keep the movement smooth. Don't come off the ramps too fast. Be ready to brake. Control it." Dwayne was adamant at giving orders, "Are you ready?"

Marianne had a note of discernment in her voice, "Hold on a minute."

Proceeding to apply red lipstick, she clearly adjusts her mirror, so her husband is visible in the side mirrors. "Ditto dear, I am ready," she finally sings smiling, as she flips her hair and enjoys her reflection in the mirror.

"Lady Luck, is with me today." Secretly smiling, her new plan unfolds before her eyes.

"Now put the car in neutral, the N." Dwayne's voice rose with concern. "KEEP YOUR FOOT ON THE BRAKE." He was puffing and short of breath from heat exhaustion.

"Hold the wheel straight; but keep your foot on the brake to control the movement. Ok, let 'er roll back, now slowly, carefully."

"Ya, ya, ya, I got it." Marianne mutters loud enough for Dwayne to hear.

"Treat me with a little respect. One more time with the brake thing and you'll get yours…"

"I will tell you when to stop." Dwayne commanded as he leaned over to adjust the driver's side ramp with the tire starting to push it off. The critical moment was quickly approaching for a successful disembarkment. The timing needed to be exactly right. The tires must roll onto the ramps, rather than push them back or up.

Marianne was tense, wriggling her foot on the brake. "My heel hurts and my foot is cramping."

Dwayne gasps to himself, "Not now, Marianne." Then hollers assurance, "It will just take a minute, cupcake, keep it coming."

Marianne completely flustered, looks down at her feet. Adjusting her right foot, it catches and her heel on her shoe breaks as she presses down on the brake.

"Sweet Lips, my heel broke, oh dear." Marianne excitedly babbles, "What am I to do?"

Lifting her shoe and foot up, broken heel in her hand, she says, "Damn, that is my favorite pair of red sling backs, the only pair I have with such lovely high heels, too." Things were not happening quite the way she envisioned in her counter plot.

Looking in the mirror she can't see Dwayne at all. Regaining her composure, she screams suddenly, "Oh, My God." She had lifted her foot off the brake when her heel broke on her shoe and her hands lifted completely off the steering wheel.

Her automobile had fallen off the trailer. Her husband's voice ran through her mind, "This is a delicate procedure and be careful. Don't take your foot off the brake."

"Oh, dear God, what have I done?"

Her horrific beast of a car stopped, as she hurriedly scurried out to survey the disaster. Hobbling on one foot, Marianne tried to put on her broken shoe with the broken heel. She saw the car's back wheel had landed right on top of Dwayne.

"Oh dear," Marianne exclaimed. "What to do, what to do?"

Going back to the vehicle to get her purse, she grabbed her cell phone. Nervous and scared, shaking badly, she misdialed the number. Listening, waiting for a 911 operator, seconds pass.

"Oh hurry, hurry," she begs into the phone. Still no response, she looks at the display "811-OO-NONONO," comes out of her mouth involuntarily as she pushes the buttons again. With great concentration, Marianne's fingers mentally acknowledge the correct number displayed on the phone. 9-1-1, finally, it rings.

"Emergency operator how may I help you?" A female voice is heard.

"Help me. No, my husband, Dwayne. Ooh, I've killed him. Oh, my God, please, there has been a terrible accident," she cried. "My husband, I drove over him. I mean a car fell on him."

Frantically, she scurries around to the back of the car. Dwayne has not moved, nor moaned, no noise, no nothing. Marianne is too disturbed to even touch him. "He looks hurt, badly injured."

She raises her voice to a squeaky frenzy. "Oh, he might be dead. He looks dead."

She continues to cry, hysterically, as the 911 emergency personnel calmly tries to figure out the location of the call. Still hopping about with one broken shoe, she moves wildly around as the 911 responder finally finishes taking down the necessary information.

Planning and wanting her spouse's demise was one thing. Participating in the actual event, aroused entirely different feelings of remorse and Marianne started to panic.

Just as the operator explains to her, "Help is on the way, remain calm, stay on the phone," a very loud thump and an agonizing cry of pain was heard.

"What happened?" The 911 dispatcher queried.

Silence. Complete silence and a clunk… Then a dead phone. Again, the question was asked. Still, no response. After relaying the information to the responders, the 911 personnel remained on a silent phone. Several minutes passed.

A young constable arrived first on the scene. He knelt on the pavement beside Marianne's lifeless body. Her upper body was outside the garage, the overhead door blocking the view to the inside scene. It crushed into her chest. A noticeable amount of blood was on her dress and pooled under her.

The rookie cop, Jim, was careful not to disturb a crime scene. He watched where he placed his hand and felt for a pulse. Nothing. Leaning over, cautious not to touch the cell phone, speaking in a very authoritative voice he states, "Constable Beech on the scene. I believe the thump heard by 911 was the garage door falling on the caller. Send backup. I am going in through the side door to check on the situation."

Although he appears lifeless, Dwayne has a pulse. The ambulance attendant waved smelling salts under his nose. Groggily, he becomes aware of many kinds of uniforms, cameras flashing, people bellowing orders and sirens. A deep male voice was inquiring, "What happened?"

Regaining his whereabouts, wearily he replies, "What do you mean what happened? The car fell on me."

Very perturbed, he answers, "Can't you see that?"

"No, uh, I am asking about the lady. Is that your wife?" A man in a formal suit, not a uniform, kneels behind the paramedic. "What happened to your wife?"

"What do you mean?" Dwayne still seems dazed by the commotion all around. "What happened? Why? Where is she? Did she take off for help? I need to see my wife!" He is close to hysterics. "Can you get this bloody car, off my leg?"

"Your wife has been knocked out, stone cold dead," the man in the suit exclaimed.

"WHAT?" Shocked, Dwayne starts to shake, face turning red.

"Get this stupid car off me. Where is she? I want to see my wife, now," he demands.

"Quiet, lie still." It was the reassuring, calm voice of the responder tending to his wounds.

"Sir, you might have a head injury from your fall or internal injuries. Please don't move."

Concerned Dwayne might go into shock; quickly the paramedic injects him with a sedative. The firemen are ready now and lift the car off him. At Royal University Hospital, Dwayne was checked over thoroughly. He wanted to be released immediately and go home. Luckily, with only sustaining injuries of a re-broken leg, a couple of broken ribs, and a few bandaged cuts and bruises on his head, he appeared relatively uninjured.

Dr. Smith declared he was one lucky mechanic. "Yes, yes, you're one extremely, lucky mechanic. Yes, you are Dwayne."

"What do you mean, lucky?" He questioned.

"It seems your wife was not as fortunate. As she was talking to the 911 dispatcher, the garage door accidentally fell on her. It was a quick way to go, with such a heavy, old door. It snapped her neck and instantly killed her."

Dwayne could barely control his tears.

"My Marianne is gone?"

The good doctor nodded. "We will keep you in the hospital a couple more days."

That was the Doc's final words, presiding over Dwayne with a large, hypodermic tranquilizer needle to help settle his nerves.

Chapter 9

THE DECISION

A much stressed Slim, walks over and puts a Barry Manilow eight track cartridge into his stereo system. He reminisces about the well-built blonde, lovely Marianne. Very well kept for her age, and extremely good-looking, but not much of a challenge though. He smiled at the recollection.

But damn! Now, only two weeks after their meeting, she dies after having taken out a huge life insurance policy on both herself and her husband. Slim was extremely concerned, aware that he had personally convinced the ditsy broad into buying a double indemnity clause not only for death, but also for disability and accidents.

Now Marianne was dead. Her mechanic husband disabled by a fallen car. What a mistake!

Applying all his smooth-talking sales techniques that day, he remembered moving in quickly on the gal, just to make a fast buck. Both were relatively young and healthy, so Slim had greedily offered his one-time payment up front for a full year, for one person and get extra free coverage for your spouse. It worked every time with the chicks.

Come into the back room and I'll cut the premiums, he'd say offering a two for one sales tactic he often used to reel in a sucker. The cheque for $1200.00 was completely valid. It had cleared the bank from their joint account with both signatures on it. Money in the bank for "Slim Hope Insurance."

Now he was screwed. It seemed he was going to have to pay out in full on both claims. The dumb dame dumped a car on her husband disabling him before she goes and drops a garage door on her own neck to get herself killed.

Frustrated by his bad luck, Slim wished that seductive blonde dame had not walked in here, that fateful day. That slow stifling hot day, cute as she was, it was a mistake. Now it was gonna cost him $2,000,000 for his cheap fling. She wasn't worth that amount of bling. No dame ever was. There was no way he was going to pay that claim; he had to get out of it somehow. It would bankrupt him.

Not able to work on anything else, going out of his mind with worry, Slim locked up the office and decided to relax and go for a drive. That might help.

Purchased years ago, while singing the lyrics to the song, "Making love in my Chevy Van," Slim's van was a white, shagging wagon from the good old teenybopper days in the 1960's. He scored quite a few times in the back of that wagon.

Does it really need a description? The license plate stated "Premium," and a modest, black lettered SLIM HOPE INSURANCE was on the side. Cruising the streets of town in his van, Slim tries to figure out how to get out of paying that policy. Being the type of person who hated to depart with any money, especially large sums, he realized he might need assistance to verify this was no accident and stop this claim.

Really, what is the chance of someone taking out a huge life insurance one week and dying the next week? How about the chances of having an accident that requires another payment, and a disability claim for the surviving spouse? Boy, if it weren't for bad luck, he would have no luck at all.

Coincidentally, a MacLean's magazine resting on his dash had a front-page article featuring Canada's finest Super Sleuth. It catches his attention. Slim picks it up. What a dandy idea.

The story sparked him to hire a private investigator for this case. It would be way cheaper than paying out that claim. It says here that this Ukrainian detective was the best female private investigator in Canada and had never lost a case.

Go figure. How about that? We have a famous detective living in our fine province of Saskatchewan, close to my home. The cover picture was worth at least a thousand words. It displayed the hottest, looking little number he'd seen in a long time. Always looking for action, Slim envisioned a sexy rendezvous with dazzling DD. He would hire the woman to solve his case but score with her as well.

Two for the incredible price of one and a real tasty treat, too. Why not? Slim was awestruck when he met DD in person. Rarely lost for words, he was finally speechless. Reading about her reputation as a fearsome sleuth was one thing. Her picture in the magazine had flaunted images that were foreign to his imagination. However, nothing prepared him for their first encounter. Her aura radiated exquisite class, elegance, and distinction, unfamiliar to a man of his breed. She was in a class of her own, a scale far exceeding anyone.

DD too, was unprepared for Slim. She couldn't believe that someone from his obsolete era still lived and breathed natural air. Something was awfully familiar about him. He was a classic, right out of an old movie or motion picture. Shades of Saturday Night Fever instantly popped in her mind.

Flabbergasted that someone with his outdated taste still lived and wore those fortrel suits. Yikes! She had never seen an authentic, original, fortrel suit. They were even worse, up close. On John Travolta they were fine, but on Slim Hope, they were just plain nasty.

Oh well, business was business and DD was always ready for a good challenge. While taking notes trying to concentrate and discuss the case, DD was crazily distracted by his white, clunky shoes. People wore those things.

"Enough, DD," quietly she chastised herself.

"Shake it off and pretend it's not real. He's only a scary, entertainment DVD."

Wait till she told Raunchy what she saw today.

Better now, more composed with her thoughts, she can take notes, concentrate on the pictures, the police report, and the insurance policy. The information is quickly registering in her personal, photographic databank.

Suddenly, DD becomes aware that the funny, horridly dressed, lecherous lizard was making a move on her. That disgusting creep. She would sic Raunchy on him later. Finishing their meeting rather abruptly, she brushes Slim off and she sends him back to his swamp.

She knows the case will be solved quickly. DD will compensate herself for his rudeness by sending him a huge bill with additional expenses.

"Hit him where it hurts the most, his pocketbook, *hroshi*, money. She would charge him double, the creep," she extrapolates.

Chapter 10

GOTCHA

After the funeral, Dwayne was laid up for a quite a while. His crushed ribs, as well as his second broken leg were a real hindrance. Needing additional surgery on his leg after the second accident crushed him. Dwayne was depressed. His leg wouldn't set properly, and he required a pin in his ankle. His life seemed bleak.

The doctor advised Dwayne not to break his leg again.

"You were lucky the car fell on your leg cast. You could have been killed too. It protected you from further damage."

"Three strikes and you're out, twice is enough."

"Right."

As if he planned to break it again; or wanted to in the first place. None of this was his plan.

"Should take a holiday." Doc says, "Rest, relax in the sun, that will help heal your leg. Stay off it."

Bored, unsure what to do with his time while his body healed, Dwayne decides to go putz around and clean up his garage. Not having been out there since that fateful accident two weeks ago, he was concerned, almost afraid. What might he find in his garage? His nerves were still shaky.

Because it was still considered a crime scene, Dwayne knew he shouldn't disturb anything but, he grumbles to himself, "What the hell! It's my garage. I will just put my tools away, that won't bother anything."

Dwayne pushes the white portion of his remote. Nothing happens, so he pushes it again. The door to the garage does not respond.

"Right, oh crap."

That's right, it had fallen. Devastated, he tries not to think about that fateful day or her. Tears form in his eyes, blurring his vision.

"Marianne, what am I going to do without my Marianne?" He cries.

Hobbling up closer to the garage, he could see the yellow police tape still spread out across the heavy steel door.

"Maybe I'll go in through the side door and fix that garage door. That should not matter or make a big difference."

Rummaging in his pocket for the key, taking out his large assortment of key rings, Dwayne picks one and slowly inserts it into the lock. Tenderly, he turns the key in the side door. Pushing it slowly, gingerly, feeling like someone or something might pounce out at him, he reaches inside the garage and he flips on the light.

The cops hadn't cleaned up anything. Two weeks later and there was still blood. Marianne's blood was still on the floor along with a white outline of where her body lay.

What was he going to do? Eyes misting over, he started to tremble. So many years they had together. They were in grade school together. He remembers pulling her pigtails. Oh, yes, he chased her across the ball diamond, caught her under the bleachers and stole the first kiss; their first kiss. He was positive she let him. She practically asked for it.

Now the tears were flowing down his red cheeks. What would he do without his only love, the love of his life? She was his beauty queen.

"Oh, Marianne, what am I going to do? I miss you already," he sniffles. "Who will get my beer on poker night?"

He regained his thoughts and proceeded to fix the garage door. Lifting the garage door from the inside, one could clearly see the problem. The release on the garage opener was unfastened from its normal housings. It really was a simple fix. As he reached up to attach it, two things occurred simultaneously; a flash of light blinded his eyes and his cell phone rang, startling Dwayne.

"Hi Dwayne."

An unrecognizable melodic, female voice was on his cell.

"My condolences to you. I guess you won't be able to go on your holiday after all. You don't know me," she teased. "But, SMILE, you're on candid camera."

"What?"

In a low, almost whispered voice DD says, "We caught you."

Startled, Dwayne hit a button on his cell and at that moment the garage door dropped down with a loud clang. Glancing at his hand, he realized his video cam was recording on his cellphone. He needed to erase it!

But standing in the side door was classy Raunchy. He quickly hustled up to Dwayne and grabs the much-needed evidence.

"Can I see that?"

Raunchy whisked the phone out of Dwayne's jerky hand, like a little kid excitedly grabbing candy. With one strong arm, he manually lifted the heavy overhead door again.

There, on the other side of the door is DD looking magnificent as usual. Wearing a smile that is larger than her white micro mini paired with tall, red, spike heeled boots. She is humming a Ukrainian polka.

"Dwayne, your jingle is right, you can fix anything. What a clever mechanic you are."

The mechanic hung his head in shame.

"You were right again, DD."

Raunchy complimented her, explaining how they caught the mechanic red-handed.

"He rigged the remote through his cell to release the garage door on his wife at the opportune moment. That's why his hand was in his pocket the whole time, in the police photographs. He was holding and hiding the evidence. Quite a clever ploy if I don't say so myself. Pre-mediated murder and almost the perfect crime!"

"*Dyakuyu*! Thank you!" says DD twirling.

Raunchy and DD, both looked spectacular in matching outfits. They look at each other at the same time and both have the exact proud smile on their faces. They really were a perfect pair!

ABOUT THE AUTHOR

Marion Mutala has a master's degree in educational administration and taught school in the K-12 system for 30 years. With a passion for the arts, she loves to write, sing, play pickle-ball and guitar, travel, and read. Marion is the author of the national bestselling and award-winning children's books, Baba's Babushka: A Magical Ukrainian Christmas, Baba's Babushka: A Magical Ukrainian Easter, Baba's Babushka: A Magical Ukrainian Wedding and Kohkum's Babushka: A Magical Metis/ Ukrainian Tale. She is also the author of Grateful, The Time for Peace is Now, Ukrainian Daughter's Dance (a poetry collection), More Baba's, Please! and My Buddy, Dido! My Dearest Dido- The Holodomor Story a book about the Ukrainian genocide is her eleventh book. Coming soon: Live Well:Ukrainian Upbringing and Other Stories and a tenth Anniversary Limited Edition hardcover collection of her Baba's Books including a new book called Baba's Babushka: A Magical Ukrainian Journey as well as a chapbook called Earth Angels/Operation Angel and her second poetry book called: Race to Finish.

Marion's awards for her children's books include:

• *Baba's Babushka: A Magical Ukrainian Christmas*

Recipient of: The Anna Pidruchney Award (2010)

• *Baba's Babushka: A Magical Ukrainian Easter*

Nominated for: Saskatchewan Book Awards – Publishing in Education (2013)

• *Baba's Babushka: A Magical Ukrainian Wedding*

Recipient of: High Plains Book Awards - Best Children's Book (2014)

• *My Buddy, Dido!*

Nominated for High Plains Book Awards Best Children's Book(2019)

Visit her website at: www.babasbabushka.ca to learn more.

Baba's Babushka: A Magical Ukrainian Wedding

Recipient of: High Plains Book Award – Best Children's Book (2014)

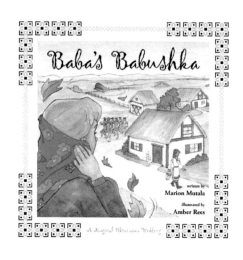

"An engrossing picture book, rendered in beautiful detail by author Marion Mutala and artist Amber Rees, that tells the heartwarming tale of a young woman named Natalia. Natalia, aided by the memory of her grandmother, goes on a magical journey to learn more about her family's – and people's – rich history. During Natalia's walk down memory lane, she visits all the important moments which involved her grandparents' time together as young people. The story details her grandparents' courtship, including the meeting of their two families before and during their seven-day Ukrainian wedding. Mutala uniquely and accurately depicts the Ukrainian customs that are special to a couple's wedding."

"Mutala's accurate portrayal of these customs will speak volumes to readers both familiar and unfamiliar with them. Her playful dialogue between the large cast of characters runs through everything, sprinkled with Ukrainian words and their meaning. Through this, she demonstrates a love of and desire to preserve the Ukrainian way of life."

Above comments from SaskBooks Review April 2014

ISBN: 9781927756065 (Published by: Your Nickel's Worth Publishing)

More Babas, Please!

"More Babas, Please! is a happy celebration of grandmothers. All grandmothers everywhere. 'Big ones, small ones, fat ones, tall. Curly-haired, straight-haired, wig-wearing, bald.' The rhyming has an almost sing-song rhythm which seems so natural that you instinctively know that a lot of work has gone into making it seem so effortless! The layout is classic and clean with lots of white space and large type, perfect for early readers and grown-ups with bad eyesight. Each left page features a beautiful full page colour illustration by Ukrainian-born illustrator Olha Tkachenko. The book gave me a warm feeling as I reflected on my own grandmother. It speaks to all the good that grandmothers do (and are) and to all the ways they surround their grandchildren with love, understanding, acceptance, affection and food!"

Comments from SaskBooks Book Review May 2017

ISBN: 9781927756928 (Published by: Your Nickel's Worth Publishing)

My Buddy, Dido!

Nominated for: High Plains Book Award – Best Children's Book (2019)

"Grandfathers are amazing people. Whether they play games, tell jokes, read stories, or simply snuggle their grandchildren, they are always sharing their love. In this delightful picture book, Mutala reminds us why grandpas are such exceptional family members."

"With her background in Ukrainian children's tales ... Mutala has a great grasp of the fundamentals, introducing readers to Dido, the Ukrainian grandfather. Before the tale even starts, a full-page graphic showcases 'grandpa' in other languages with bright, bold colours."

"Marion also strays from the regular story format, choosing instead to go over a Dido's characteristics in rhyming verses: "Who listens to me when I'm mad? Who consoles me when I'm sad? Who has time when I'm in a pickle or when I'm ready for a tickle?" Every facet of a grandfather is explored in poetry sure to appeal both the young and old."

Comments from SaskBooks review August 2018.

ISBN: 9781988783239 (Published by: Your Nickel's Worth Publishing)

Kohkum's Babushka: A Magical Métis/Ukrainian Tale

This is a tale about two diverse families and their first encounter with one another. It shows the beauty of their differences and similarities, particularly the generosity and reciprocity valued by each family's cultural tradition. Through another magical Babushka, Marion Mutala takes readers into a vibrant Prairie world that weaves fact and fantasy to witness two families, one Métis and the other Ukrainian, meeting for the first time. Through this magical encounter, we see core values intrinsic to our common humanity: our curiosity and empathy, and our willingness to share with others, regardless of language or culture.

ISBN: 978192679578-2 (Published by: Gabriel Dumont Institute Press)

Baba's Babushka: A Magical Ukrainian Easter

Nominated for: Saskatchewan Book Award – Publishing in Education (2013)

"This enchanting sequel to the award-winning Baba's Babushka: A Magical Ukrainian Christmas is sure to delight Marion Mutala's many fans. This time it's spring, and we join Natalia as she is once again swept magically away to a far-off land for another uniquely Ukrainian adventure.

Natalia is sent outside while the paska, the Easter bread her mother is baking, rises. She's meant to be collecting the eggs but instead finds herself reflecting on her beloved Baba, her grandmother, who has recently died. Suddenly she feels raindrops brush her cheeks. The raindrops turn into a babushka that covers her hair and then she's off... "up and away, high in the sky... racing through time and space". Natalia finds herself in a crowd of people in the early morning in front of a village church. It's Easter and Natalia is caught up in the celebrations as she joins the procession of people carrying candles..."

The book is easy-to-read with beautiful full-page illustrations by Saskatchewan illustrator Wendy Siemens.

Comments from SaskBooks review April 2013.

ISBN: 978-1894431705 (Published by: Your Nickel's Worth Publishing)

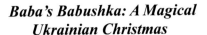
Baba's Babushka: A Magical Ukrainian Christmas

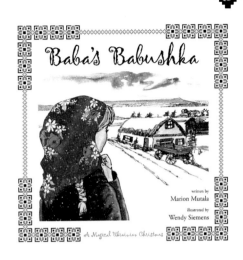

Recipient of: The Anna Pidruchney Award (2010)

"Saskatchewan author Marion Mutala has created a charming story that celebrates her proud Ukrainian heritage and lives up to the subtitle of her book, 'A Magical Ukrainian Christmas'. Natalia, the star of this lively story, is a little Ukrainian girl living in rural Saskatchewan who is taken, with the reader, on an enchanted journey back in time. Although Natalia is excited, like all children, about Christmas, her joy is marred by a deep sadness. This will be the first Christmas that her beloved grandmother, Baba, will not be present to share in the fun, festivities, and traditions of Christmas with her family. One day, a brightly coloured red and blue babushka, or headscarf, appears out of nowhere that reminds Natalia of the one her Baba used to wear. Mysteriously transported to another time and place, Natalia finds herself sharing a meal with a strangely familiar family who perform all the same Christmas Eve traditions her own family does....

Natalia is just as magically transported back to the present and her own home.... She finds a picture of her Baba on the table beside her bed with the red and blue babushka tucked underneath it. Who was the little girl she spent Christmas Eve with? Could it have been her own dear Baba?"

Comments from SaskBooks review January 2011.

ISBN: 9781894431538 (Published by: Your Nickel's Worth Publishing)

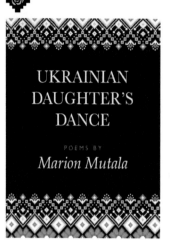

Ukrainian Daughter's Dance

The rich and varied poems in Ukrainian Daughter's Dance speak to the heart as they document a woman's life journey, as a Ukrainian-Canadian, and as a prairie woman, and her voyage of self-discovery. Her story can be anyone's story. Poems explore issues of immigrant identity and voice in the prairies, and celebrate a cultural heritage expressed through song, dance, art, work and life.

ISBN: 9781771333337 (Published by: Inanna Publications)

My Dearest Dido

The Holodomor Story

The Holodomor Story
Marion Mutala

"Simply because they were Ukrainian! My Dearest Dido-The Holodomor Story is a haunting account of the innocent victims of Stalin's vicious regime. In the name of communism, Stalin, and his armed units branded Ukrainians traitors and tortured, beat, starved, and shot them -often for the simple crime of eating stocks of grain.

This heart-breaking record is based on the voices of survivors and told through the eyes of Dido Bohdan and his granddaughter, Hanusia. The Holodomor or Great Ukrainian Famine was a five-year plan engineered by Stalin that starved millions of people. Stalin attempted to control Ukraine by destroying families, crushing communities, silencing media, and eradicating Ukrainian culture.

The victims of the Holodomor are remembered!

Ukrainian candles burn brightly. Their flames will not be extinguished. "

ISBN 9781989078204 (Published by: Wood Dragon Books)

ABOUT THE ARTIST

Ukrainian-born Olha Tkachenko is the artist behind the cover art of The Mechanic's Wife. She was also the illustrator for four previous books by Marion Mutala: My Dearest Dido-The Holodomor Story, More Babas, Please! and My Buddy, Dido! and Baba's Babushka: A Magical Journey to Kyiv.

Since 2008, Olha has worked as a freelance children's illustrator and has created many children books in the USA, Canada, and Russia. In 2014, Olha and her family moved to Canada, where she worked at the Ukrainian Museum of Canada in Saskatchewan and led a private art school. Her work has been exhibited in Ukraine, France, and Canada.

Olha works with various media such as oil, soft pastel, watercolors, and batiks. Her hot batik works combine traditional Ukrainian techniques of Pysankas (painted Easter Eggs) and modern concepts.

Reviewers have stated that Tkachenko adds a fantastical element to the stories she illustrates with her watercolour inspired illustrations. SaskBook reviewers claim her "simplicity and splashes of colour are both childlike and detailed, an absolute necessity if you want to hold your reader's attention".

Olha says, "I love tales where a line between reality and imagination is almost erased, like in childhood. If we ask children about miracles, they might deny this idea, but even the desire to look smart and adult would not stop a child from peering into the grass near the path to see a gnome or a fairy.

Likewise, I love peering into reality looking for a mystery. Therefore, I'd call my style realistic fantasy. My favourite medium - coloured pencils - expresses my feelings in the best way. My drawings are full of colours and air. They breathe and the white light leaks out through the net of small pencil strokes, just as grace is tangible through the ordinary things in our habitual, material world."

Find out more about her work at: https://www.olyaillustrations.com or www.olya-t.art